THE WRONG KIND OF BARK

WRITTEN BY **Julia Donaldson**

ILLUSTRATED BY **Garry Parsons**

For Hamish and Jeddah

J.D.

For Christopher and Emma

G.P.

EGMONT

We bring stories to life

Book Band: Gold

Lexile® measure: 470L

First published in Great Britain 2004
This Reading Ladder edition published 2016
by Egmont UK Limited
The Yellow Building, 1 Nicholas Road, London W11 4AN
Text copyright © Julia Donaldson 2004
Illustrations copyright © Garry Parsons 2004
The author and illustrator have asserted their moral rights
ISBN 978 1 4052 8237 6
www.egmont.co.uk
A CIP catalogue record for this title is available from the British Library.
Printed in Singapore
34940/18

Series consultant: Nikki Gamble

Chapters

Reading Ladder

Finlay and the Fish

Finlay sat next to the fish tank. He liked watching the fish. They were more interesting than the teacher.

There was a little bridge at the bottom of the fish tank. But the fish never swam under it. Or maybe they did when Finlay wasn't looking.

The big fish was swimming very near the bridge now.

'Go on!' Finlay whispered. 'Swim under it!'

The teacher was talking to the class. 'Tomorrow, I want you all to bring in a flower for the nature table,' she said. 'It can be any kind of flower.'

Finlay watched the big fish. It swam over the bridge.

'Finlay!' said the teacher. 'What did I just say?'

'Any kind of flower,' said Finlay.

'Yes,' said the teacher. 'And stop staring at the fish!'

The Wrong Kind of Flower

'Did you all remember to bring in a flower?'
asked the teacher next day.

Most of the class had.

Sally Wong had a marigold.

David Simmons had a rose. A lot of it had been eaten by greenfly.

Ruth Goodchild had a pansy. She had some extra flowers for the teacher too.

I grew it myself.

The teacher filled a jam jar with water. She put it on the nature table. 'Now, all put your flowers in here,' she said.

Sally Wong put in the marigold.

David Simmons put in what was left of
the rose.

Ruth Goodchild put in the pansy.

'Please, Miss,' she said. 'Look what
Finlay's doing.'

The teacher looked at Finlay. He was
pouring some white stuff out of a bag into
the water.

'What are you doing, Finlay?' asked
the teacher.

'Putting my flour in the water, like you said,
Miss,' said Finlay.

'That's the wrong kind of flour,' said the teacher. She had to change the water.

13

Later on, Finlay was watching the fish again. The little one was swimming very near the bridge.

'Go on!' whispered Finlay. 'Swim under it!'

The teacher was talking to the class. 'Tomorrow, I want you all to bring in a nut for the nature table,' she said. 'It can be any kind of nut.'

Finlay watched the little fish. It swam around the bridge.

'Finlay!' said the teacher. 'What did I just say?'

'Any kind of nut,' said Finlay.

'Yes,' said the teacher. 'And stop staring at the fish!'

The Wrong Kind of Nut

'Did you all remember to bring in a nut?'
asked the teacher next day.

Most of the class had.

Sally Wong had
a walnut.

David Simmons
had a conker. It
had got a bit
broken in a fight.

Ruth Goodchild
had a coconut.
She had a packet
of peanuts for the
teacher too.

'Now, put them all on the nature table,'
said the teacher.

Sally Wong put down the walnut.

David Simmons put down the
broken conker.

Miss!
Miss!

Ruth Goodchild
put down the
coconut.

'Please, Miss,' she
said. 'Finlay's putting
some metal things on
the table. That's not
what you said, Miss,
is it?'

'What are those, Finlay?' said the teacher.

'They're nuts, like you said, Miss,' said
Finlay. 'My dad was screwing some into some
shelves and he let me have these ones.'

'That's the wrong
kind of nut,' said
the teacher.

She moved
Finlay to a
different table.
'Now you can
stop staring at
the fish,'
she said.

Try and
concentrate,
Finlay.

'Right,' said the teacher. 'It's time to practise our play.'

The class was doing a play about nature. Some children had made masks.

Sally Wong had a daisy mask.

Finlay had a tomato mask.

David Simmons had a yellow mask. He was being the sun. He had cut one eye bigger than the other, but the teacher said it didn't matter.

Hey, Tomato face!

Some children were being raindrops. They had long paper ribbons tied to their arms. The ribbons were supposed to be the rain.

Ruth Goodchild was Mother Nature. She had a wand and was allowed to boss everybody about.

Stop raining!

The children practised the play in the hall.
Then they came back to the classroom.

Finlay's new table was by the window.
There was some scaffolding up outside. Some
builders were going to do some work on the
school roof. They were sitting on the
scaffolding having their lunch. One of them
had dropped a bit of his sandwich. A bird was
hopping towards it.

'Go on,' whispered Finlay. 'Get it!'

The teacher was talking to the class.

'I want you all to bring in part of a tree for the nature table,' she said. 'It can be a twig, or a leaf, or a little bit of bark.'

Finlay watched the bird. It flew away.

'Finlay!' said the teacher. 'What did I just say?'

'Bring in bark,' said Finlay.

'Yes,' said the teacher. 'And stop staring out of the window.'

The Wrong Kind of Bark

The teacher came into the classroom the next day.

There were a lot of children round Finlay's table.

Miss!
Miss!

25

'Please, Miss,' said Ruth Goodchild.
'Finlay's got a dog. That's not what you said, Miss, is it?'

Finlay had a small puppy in his arms.

'Finlay, you can't bring pets to school,' said the teacher.

'But you said to bring in a bark, Miss,' said
Finlay. The puppy barked loudly.

'That's the wrong kind of bark,' said the
teacher.

She phoned Finlay's home to see if his
mum or dad could come for the puppy.
But no one was in.

The teacher went back into the classroom.

The puppy was standing on the nature table. He was barking at the builders.

The jar of flowers was on its side. Most of the nuts were on the floor.

'Take him off the table, Finlay,' said the teacher. She cleared up the mess.

The puppy
went on and on
barking at the
builders. Finlay
put his anorak
under the
nature table.

'What are you
doing now,
Finlay?' asked
the teacher.

'I'm making
a bed for the
puppy,' said
Finlay. The
puppy lay down
on the anorak.
He stopped
barking.

'Now it's time to do the play for the rest of the school,' said the teacher.

The children put on their masks.

Sally Wong put on her daisy mask.

It's hot in here.

David Simmons put on his sun mask.

Finlay put on his tomato mask.

How do I tie this?

The puppy started to bark again. He barked and barked at the tomato mask.

'He doesn't like the tomato mask,' said Finlay. 'He thinks it's attacking me.'

'Take the mask off,' said the teacher. 'You can put it on when we're down in the hall.'

Finlay took off
the tomato mask.
The puppy
growled. He
grabbed the mask
in his mouth and
tore it up.

Stop it!

The teacher was very cross. 'I'll have to tie
him up,' she said. She
found some string.
She tied one end of
it to the puppy's
collar. Then she
tied the other
end round a leg
of Finlay's table.

Finlay had to make a new tomato mask.
There wasn't time for the paint to dry.

The teacher put the paint pot up on a
shelf. Then they went down to the hall to act
the play to the rest of the school.

The puppy was left alone in the classroom.

The builders were banging on the roof. The puppy barked at them. The builders went on banging. The shelves on the wall started to shake. They shook and shook. The pot of red paint jumped on the shelf. It fell on its side. The red paint started to run out of it . . .

Tomato Trouble

Down in the hall the children were doing their play. The children being flowers and fruit were curled up on the stage.

Ruth Goodchild was sitting in a chair with tinsel tied on it. It was her throne. 'Pitter patter raindrops,' she said. She waved her wand.

The children being raindrops ran on to the stage. They shook the ribbons on their arms. They were supposed to be watering the flowers and fruit.

David Simmons came on to the stage in his sun mask. He stood stiffly over the plants. From far off came a barking sound.

'Grow, plants, grow,' said Ruth.

The children being flowers and fruit began to uncurl. Finlay uncurled. The red paint from his tomato mask dripped down his t-shirt.

Grow, plants, grow.

The barking grew louder and louder.

'Grow taller,' said Ruth.

The flowers and fruit grew. Most of them grew slowly.

But the tomato shot up. It was still dripping red paint. The tomato jumped off the stage. It ran through the hall and up the stairs.

Ruth Goodchild looked cross.

I said **grow**, not go!

The Right Kind of Bark

The teacher went out of the hall. Quietly, she followed the tomato up the stairs.

Finlay went into the classroom. The teacher followed him.

What's going on?

42

The puppy had stopped barking at the
builders. He was barking at the fish tank.
He was barking and barking and barking.

On the shelf the pot of red paint lay on its side. Red paint was running out of it. A few drops had dripped into the fish tank.

'Quick!' said the teacher. 'Bring me a jam jar of water, Finlay.' She took the paint pot off the shelf and put it on her table.

There was a net next to the fish tank. The teacher fished the big fish out of the tank.

Finlay and the puppy watched. The puppy had stopped barking.

The teacher tried to fish out the little fish. But it was a very fast swimmer. It kept swimming away.

'Yes!' said Finlay. The little fish was swimming under the bridge!

The teacher held the net the other side of the bridge and the little fish swam into it.

The teacher took the fish into the classroom next door. They had a fish tank too. She put the fish in it.

CLASS THREE'S FISH

'Now we'll have to change the water in our tank,' she said. 'We can't have the fish swallowing red paint.'

Later on, the other children came back to the classroom.

Ruth Goodchild still looked cross.

'I'm sorry I missed the end of the play,' said the teacher. 'But in a way I'm glad. If all the paint had gone into the water, the fish could be dead. What a good thing that Finlay's puppy warned us.'

Finlay cuddled his puppy.

'Perhaps it was the right kind of bark after all,' he said.